I Am
Spider-Man

🎬 HarperCollins*Entertainment*

COLUMBIA PICTURES PRESENTS A MARVEL ENTERPRISES PRODUCTION A LAURA ZISKIN PRODUCTION "SPIDER-MAN"
STARRING: TOBEY MAGUIRE WILLEM DAFOE KIRSTEN DUNST JAMES FRANCO CLIFF ROBERTSON ROSEMARY HARRIS
MUSIC BY DANNY ELFMAN EXECUTIVE PRODUCERS AVI ARAD STAN LEE SCREENPLAY BY DAVID KOEPP BASED ON THE MARVEL COMIC BOOK BY STAN LEE PRODUCED BY LAURA ZISKIN IAN BRYCE DIRECTED BY SAM RAIMI

MARVEL
sony.com/Spider-Man
COLUMBIA
PICTURES

First published in the USA by HarperFestival, a division of HarperCollins*Publishers* in 2002
First published in Great Britain by HarperCollins*Entertainment* in 2002

HarperCollins*Entertainment* is an imprint of
HarperCollins*Publishers* Ltd, 77-85 Fulham Palace Road,
Hammersmith, London W6 8JB

The HarperCollins website address is
www.**fire**and**water**.com

1 3 5 7 9 8 6 4 2
ISBN 0 00 713798 2

Printed and bound in Great Britain by Scotprint

GO FOR THE ULTIMATE SPIN AT
www.sony.com/Spider-Man

I Am Spider-Man

Adaptation by Acton Figueroa
Based on the screenplay by David Koepp
Illustrations by Ron Lim
Coloring by Emily Y. Kanalz

HarperCollins*Entertainment*
An Imprint of HarperCollins*Publishers*

Maybe you've heard of me.

Maybe you've seen me.

I am Spider-Man.

I wasn't always a superhero.
I used to be a regular guy,
just like everyone else.
Well, not exactly like
everyone else.

I was sort of a geek.

I really liked school.

But it wasn't always easy for me.

I didn't always fit in.

Some of the kids didn't like me.

Everything changed

when we went on a field trip

to learn about spiders.

Man-made spiders. Super-spiders.

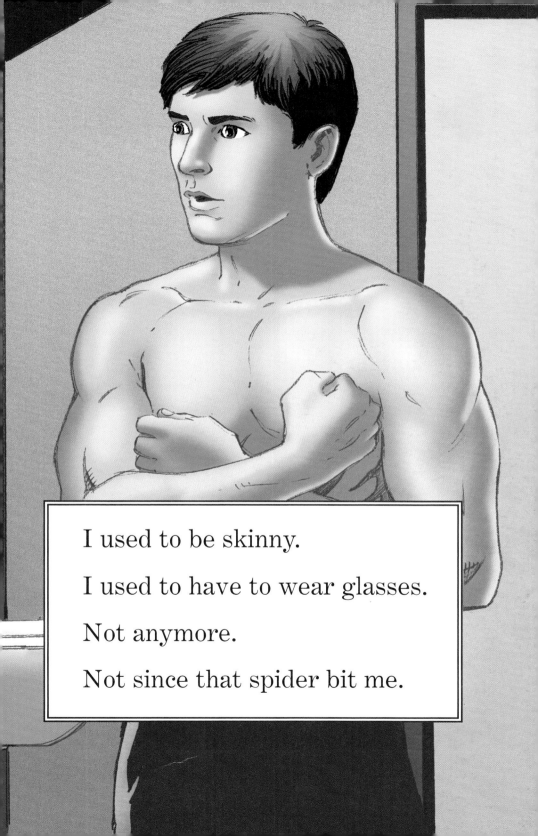

I used to be skinny.

I used to have to wear glasses.

Not anymore.

Not since that spider bit me.

Now I am fast.

Now I am strong.

I don't like to fight,
but sometimes I have no choice.

The kids at school were amazed at my new strength.

Like the spider that bit me,
I have an extra sense.
My spider sense warns me
when someone needs my help.

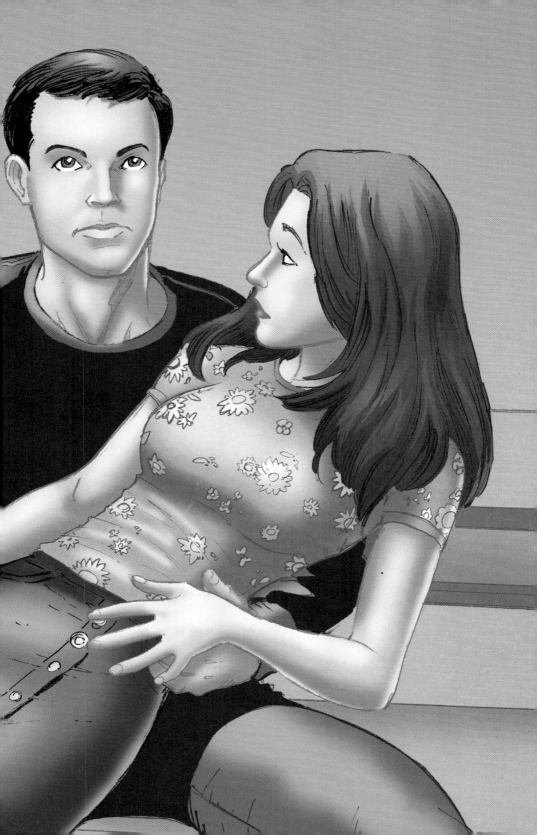

After the spider bit me,
I began to make webbing.
At first I couldn't control it.

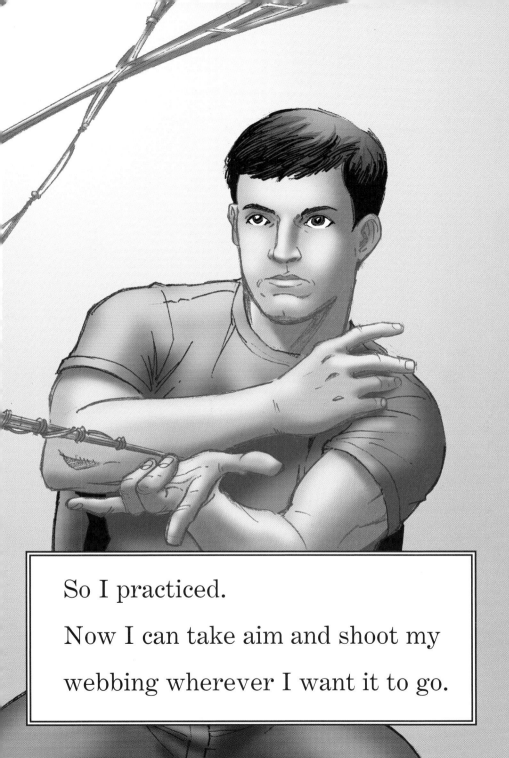

So I practiced.

Now I can take aim and shoot my webbing wherever I want it to go.

I swore to use my powers
to help the people of this city.
But I had to protect myself.
If the bad guys knew who I was,
my family would be in danger.

And so I became Spider-Man.

Like a spider, I can climb walls.

My fingers can stick to anything.

I can swing through the city
on a strand of webbing.

I can flip, dip, and whirl.

I am strong enough
to fight four bad guys at once!

I can go places no one else can.

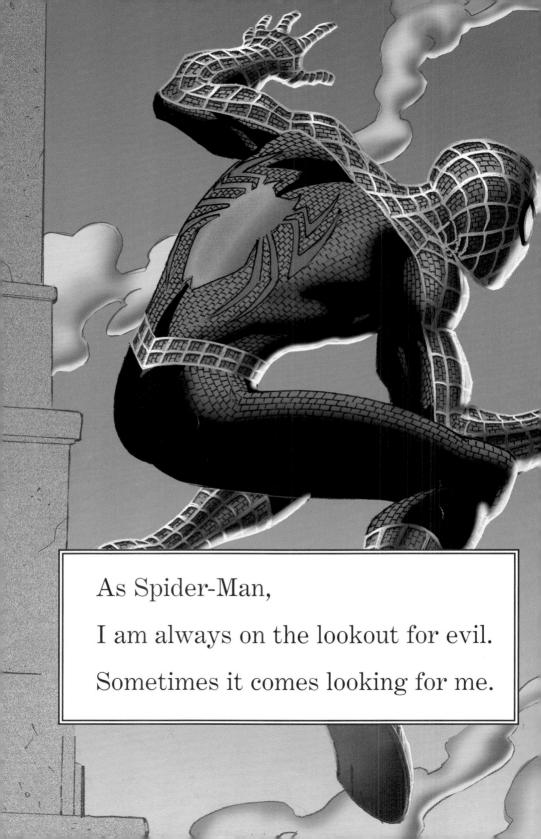

As Spider-Man,

I am always on the lookout for evil.

Sometimes it comes looking for me.

I'll always be Peter Parker.
But when people are in danger,
I *am* Spider-Man.